THE CONDOR

BY
LISA WESTBERG PETERS

EDITED BY
JULIE BACH

CRESTWOOD HOUSE
New York

LIBRARY OF CONGRESS CATALOGING IN PUBLICATION DATA

Peters, Lisa Westberg.
  The condor

  (Wildlife, habits & habitat)
  Includes index.
  SUMMARY: Describes the physical characteristics and behavior of the condor.
Includes a map of the birds' natural habitat.
  1. Condors—Juvenile literature.   [1. Condors.]   I. Title.   II. Series.
QL696.F33P48   1990   598'.912—dc20   89-28270
ISBN 0-89686-515-0

PHOTO CREDITS:

Cover: Photo Researchers: Ron Austing
Photo Researchers: (Tom McHugh) 4, 13, 15, 17; (Frank Schreider) 10, 45
Berg & Associates: (Warren Jacobi) 8, 12, 38
Journalism Services: (Mark Gamba) 18
Zoological Society of San Diego: 9, 21, 29, 37; (Ron Garrison) 23, 27, 33, 35, 43: (F.D.
  Schmidt) 24

CRESTWOOD HOUSE

Macmillan Publishing Company
866 Third Avenue
New York, NY 10022
Collier Macmillan Canada, Inc.

Printed in the United States of America
First Edition
10 9 8 7 6 5 4 3 2 1

TABLE OF CONTENTS

A California condor soars above Los Padres National Forest in California.

INTRODUCTION:

Here are two scenes from the past:

A cattle rancher looks out over his land in southern California. All around him lies dry grassland dotted with thickets of green shrubs—*chaparral* country. A mountain range looms in the distance.

The wind is the only sound. Just then, he hears a whistling sound. A shadow passes over him. A huge bird flies overhead. The bird isn't flapping its wings. It is just soaring in the wind.

The bird seems to know where it is going. Soon, the rancher sees the bird snap its great wings above its head, flap them rapidly, and drop out of the sky.

The bird joins a flock of others just like it. They are feasting on the *carcass* of a deer.

The rancher watches the birds share the meal. They pull and tear at the soft flesh. In time, the birds fly away, heavy with their meal. Almost nothing is left of the deer.

* * *

On another continent, it is time for a fiesta. South American Indian villagers capture a large bird.

They bring the bird back to the village and sew its feet to the shoulders of a bull. Everyone watches while the two animals careen around the courtyard for a short time until the bull grows tired. In a day or two, the villagers release the bird.

The people think of the bird as a symbol of themselves. The bull is a symbol of the Spanish conquerors. The struggle of the two animals represents a triumph of the Indian spirit over the Spanish many years ago.

* * *

The birds in both of these cases are condors. The first is the California condor. The second is the Andean condor. They are members of the vulture family. Both are *endan-*

■ Range of the California condor

▨ Range of the Andean condor

gered. Few of these birds exist and their lives are threatened in their natural environment.

But people's relationship to condors has changed. *Biologists* captured the last wild California condor in 1987. They brought it to San Diego, where half of the tiny population now lives.

If scientists succeed in breeding enough healthy California condors, this symbol of freedom and wilderness will return to the California skies.

And in the Andes Mountains of South America, the traditional Indian ceremonies are now illegal. The Andean condor, the largest vulture in the world, still flies free, and the government is trying to expand its range.

But condors are still not safe. They face many threats from people.

CHAPTER ONE:

The ancient Incas of Peru thought the condor carried the sun into the sky each morning. They considered it a messenger to the gods.

It is no mystery why people long ago believed that the bird had special powers. With wings as large and strong as the condor's, a trip into the clouds is easy.

The Andean condor can be identified by the white patches on the top sides of its wings.

Built to soar

Both the Andean condor and the California condor are New World vultures in the Cathartides family. The condor's name comes from *kuntur*, a native South American word.

Scientists call the Andean condor *Vultur gryphus*. Its wingspan is ten feet across.

The California condor is called *Gymnogyps califor-nianus*. In Greek, *gymnos* means naked, *gyps* means vulture. Its wingspan is nine or ten feet. It is the largest land bird in North America.

Both types of condors are mostly black. The California condor has white patches on the underside of its wings. The Andean condor has white patches on the top side.

The California condor's feathers are black like the Andean condor's, but its white patches are on the undersides of its wings.

Both condors are powerful fliers and perhaps the most graceful soaring birds on earth. An observer half a mile away can hear the bird flapping its wings. If the condor is soaring overhead, an observer can hear the wind whistle through its feathers.

The condor can soar for an hour or more without flapping. But it must find good *thermals*, or warm updrafts of air. It can fly thousands of feet above the ground and up to 60 miles per hour. It can fly hundreds of miles a day searching for food.

Condors have long flight feathers at the tips of their wings. The feathers make up almost a third of the length of the wing and are longer than a human forearm. The feathers spread like fingers. They help prevent stalling by responding to changes in the wind. The tail feathers are used for braking and steering.

Graceful in the air, condors are a bit clumsy on the ground. At 20 to 30 pounds, they are slow to lift off the ground, especially if they have just eaten a large meal. They have to hop, run, and flap their wings to take off.

Sometimes, the condor walks uphill before lifting off to save itself the trouble of flapping its wings. In the past, people took advantage of that clumsy moment to capture the bird.

Warm updrafts of air lift this Andean condor high above the mountains of Chile.

The black ruff and red-orange head of the California condor

The head of a scavenger

Condors are *scavengers*. They prefer to eat dead meat —and that can be messy. To make the clean-up job easier, condors have bald heads with no feathers to get matted down. Condors often bathe in mountain streams or wipe their heads in the grass or sand after eating.

The California condor's head is red-orange with a black *ruff*. Males and females look exactly alike. The only way to tell them apart is with a blood test or surgery.

The Andean condor's head is purplish black with a white ruff. The male has a fleshy comb on top, the same

The head of the Andean condor, like that of the California condor, has no feathers.

color as its head. Both types of condors can draw their featherless heads into their ruffs to keep warm.

Both male and female California condors have red eyes. The female Andean condor has red eyes and the male has brown eyes.

Condors have excellent eyesight, which helps them find food. Some say their eyesight is seven times as good as human eyesight. In some villages in South America, people used to roast and eat condors' eyes because they believed the eyes would improve their own eyesight.

Condors have no sense of smell. Sometimes they rely on their cousin, the turkey vulture, to sniff out carcasses.

No head of a scavenging bird is complete without a strong beak to tear meat apart. The hooked upper beak is pale in color.

Flat feet

An eagle must be able to grasp living *prey* with its feet. To do this, it has *talons* that are as sharp as needles.

Because condors don't need to catch and hold live prey, their feet are almost flat. They hold onto carcasses with long, scaly toes while they pull at the meat with their strong beaks.

A condor's feet are like a turkey's. They are designed for walking, not for grasping and killing.

There are no confirmed reports of a California condor

The feet of the California and the Andean condors (above) end in scaly toes and are used for walking, not grasping or killing.

attacking live prey. South Americans, however, tell of the Andean condor attacking newborn calves or goats. It is clear, though, that condors are better designed to scavenge than to hunt.

15

An unattractive bird?

The condor, like all vultures, has some unpleasant habits and a few ugly features. For example, the condor's bald head is not especially attractive to most people, but it helps the bird to keep clean. And its habit of eating the rotting flesh of dead animals repels some people.

But vultures are filling an important *niche* in the environment. By eating dead meat, they clean up the land and get rid of possible sources of disease. Carcasses attract flies and other insects that are more likely than condors to carry disease.

A condor hisses when it is competing for its share of a carcass. It's an unpleasant sound. The birds hiss because they have no vocal cords. Scientists think they are voiceless because they don't attack live prey and therefore don't defend a territory. The birds don't need voices to announce their presence to other animals.

Condors also defecate down the sides of their legs. This, too, serves a purpose. Because condors have no sweat glands, they expel their feces on their legs. The liquid evaporates and the birds cool off.

Condors, like other vultures, vomit when they are frightened. People associate vomiting with sickness. But for condors, it is a useful habit. A condor often overeats. If a bird needs to escape quickly after a meal, it will vomit to lose weight and takeoff becomes easier.

16

Condors may not be pretty birds up close, but soaring above the mountains, they are spectacular.

CHAPTER TWO:

The condor is an ancient *species*. Its ancestors can be traced back 60 million years.

The condor family also boasts the largest flying bird ever. In glacial deposits in Nevada, scientists found fossil remains of *Teratornis incredibilis*, which means "unbelievable bird monster." The bird had a 16- to 17-foot wingspan.

**Teratornis incredibilis*, the condor's early ancestor, was a huge bird that lived 60 million years ago.*

Mountain life

The California condor's ancestors used to fly across much of North America. The American explorers Meriwether Lewis and William Clark saw California condors in the Columbia River basin.

In South America, the Andean condor used to fly along the entire length of the Andes Mountains and often down to the coast.

The condor's *range* is much smaller today. For the past several decades, the California condor's range was limited to a horseshoe-shaped area of mountains around the San Joaquin Valley in southern California.

It preferred the rugged mountain areas for nesting and *roosting*. It liked desert canyons and dry grasslands for *foraging*.

The Andean condor is often restricted to the highest, most rugged parts of the mountains from Venezuela to Tierra del Fuego, at the tip of South America.

Finding food

Thousands of years ago, the condor's ancestors probably fed on the carcasses of *mammals* such as saber-toothed tigers and woolly mammoths.

Today's condor feeds instead on the carcasses of ranch animals such as cattle, sheep, goats, and horses. It also

The condor's range has become extremely limited as more and more land has been developed.

feeds on dead deer, squirrels, and rabbits. The California condor used to feed on the carcasses of whales and sea mammals on the sea coast.

The Andean condor still feeds on dead sea mammals, which helps to keep the shores clean. It also raids the nests of sea birds, such as the cormorant and the pelican, on islands off the coast of Peru. The eggs provide a tasty meal.

The people of Peru use the droppings of the birds to make fertilizer. They used to shoot many condors in the belief that the big birds threatened the population of the sea birds.

Now it is illegal to shoot condors in Peru and other South American countries. Today, scientists think that the condors help control the sea bird population, not endanger it.

Because they are vultures, condors can eat diseased and infected meat and not be harmed by it. They have special bacteria in their digestive tracts that break down toxic, or poisonous, germs.

When California condors lived in the wild, people might have seen 10 or 20 of them gathered around a carcass. The big birds sometimes shared their meals with crows, ravens, and turkey vultures. Eagles were usually able to drive a condor from a carcass.

Condors stuff themselves when they find a carcass. After a large meal, they might not eat for several days.

Finding a mate

At about age five, the California condor's adult *plumage* is complete. It can mate at age six or seven. The Andean condor can mate at about age eight. Condors court each other between December and February.

The mating ritual for the Andean and California condors is similar. The male usually shows off for the female. He spreads his wings, lowers his head, and struts. He faces the female, then may turn his back to her with wings spread, tail dragging. The male might repeat this display several times.

The female may seem unimpressed or annoyed at the

This male California condor spreads his wings and lowers his head to court the female.

display. She might even peck at the male's neck. But mating usually takes place after the courtship display.

Scientists believe the condor mates for life. Evidence suggests that condors will use the same nest for years if they are not disturbed.

Barely a nest

If the pair does not already have a nest site, it selects one together.

A condor nest is hardly worthy of the name. When most people think of a nest, they think of a round object made of sticks or mud or grass. Condors don't bother building one. They simply pick out a sheltered spot on a cliff or in a cave high in the mountains. Sometimes they choose the hollow of a tree.

The spot must have room for both adults and for the young bird. It must have good roosting perches nearby. And it must have an easy approach from the air and protection from storms and wind.

Condors have been known to abandon nesting areas if human activity disturbs them over a long period. Even a hiking trail can disturb nesting condors.

Condors are fussy about their nesting sites and prefer sheltered spots. This young California condor is living in a large hole in a hollow tree.

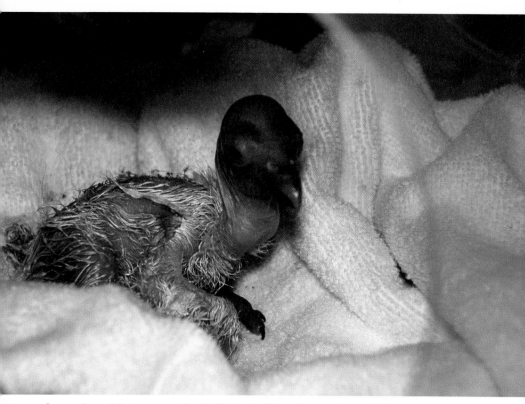

A condor chick grows fast. This California condor chick was hatched successfully in captivity.

A long childhood

The female condor lays a single egg, usually in February or March. The Andean condor's egg is white. The California condor's egg is pale blue or green. The eggs are about four and a half inches by two and a half inches.

Both parents share the job of sitting on the egg. Later, they both help to raise the chick.

The egg hatches in April or May. The chick is covered with grayish down. When it is about three months old, it gets its first feathers.

The parents feed the chick by *regurgitating* food. The chick thrusts its head into the parent's mouth to make the parent release food. The heads of the parent and chick pump back and forth as the chick eats.

A chick has a huge appetite and it grows fast. It can gain up to 10 percent of its body weight in one day.

By the time the chick is about six months old, its feathers are in and it is ready to fly. The young California condor remains a dull black until its shiny black adult feathers come in. The young Andean condor is brown.

The parents keep feeding the chick throughout the fall and winter. In fact, the chick stays dependent on the adults for up to two years. Because of this, condors in the wild lay only one egg every other year. It would be too hard to take care of a *fledgling* and an egg at the same time.

Condors are long-lived if their *habitat* is safe. No one knows precisely how long condors live in the wild, but they have lived nearly 50 years in captivity.

CHAPTER THREE:

People have been shooting condors for as long as they have had guns. Unlike Native Americans, who considered the condor magical, American settlers thought the huge bird was a threat. They believed the birds carried away calves and children. A man would shoot a condor and brag about it to his friends.

Target practice

There are many stories of American pioneers killing condors. In 1854, a pony express rider found one asleep near his cabin. He struck the bird with a shovel and broke its wing.

Legend has it that gold miners killed the birds for their huge quills. They filled the quills, a half-inch in diameter, with gold dust and corked the open ends with pieces of wood.

People also killed condors simply because vultures were unpopular. Settlers thought condors spread disease because they ate the infected meat of dead animals. Scientists have found no evidence for that. But one hundred years ago, people did not know much about the bird.

The state of California passed a law in the 1880s that made it illegal to shoot a condor. But if people knew about the law, they paid little attention to it. Very few people were ever punished for the crime.

In modern times, people kept shooting condors despite the growing evidence that the birds were not harmful.

Collectors' items

In the wild, the condor's slow pace of laying eggs also worked against the bird.

Making matters worse, people used to collect condor eggs. They drained the contents of the eggs and bought and sold the eggs like treasured antiques. Collectors sometimes paid hundreds of dollars for a condor egg.

Once an egg is laid in captivity, zookeepers keep a close eye on its development. Here, a zookeeper carefully weighs the delicate egg that contains Molloko, a California condor.

Between 1859 and 1943, at least 70 condor eggs were collected. Many of them were placed in natural history museum collections.

Some scientists believe that breeding pairs of condors broke up and stopped producing eggs when egg collectors repeatedly raided their nests.

People also collected condor skins, often to fill out museum collections.

A poisoned, shrinking home

For years, California ranchers used poisoned bait to kill animals that they saw as threats to their cattle or sheep. They often killed coyotes and ground squirrels.

People suspected condors also died from the poisons because they ate the carcasses of the dead animals. They knew ravens, hawks, eagles, and turkey vultures could die from eating poisoned meat or grain. But some people said the condor was safe from the poisons because of its ability to eat diseased meat.

After more years of study, it became clear that the poison set out for coyotes and squirrels could also kill condors. Now poisoned bait is illegal in California.

Condors faced other problems. Use of the pesticide DDT resulted in thin condor egg shells. The thin shells broke early instead of hatching. Condors also died from

Because the California condor's range is shrinking, scientists now capture the wild condors and protect them in captivity.

lead poisoning after eating animals shot with lead bullets.

Besides the dangers of poison, condors faced the threat of development. People started building roads and trails and aqueducts in the condor's nesting areas. They started drilling for oil and gas. They came into the forests to cut lumber.

Areas safe for the condor to raise its young shrank. A bird with no natural *predators* was finding it hard to compete against its new enemy—people.

Attempts to save the condor

In the 1930s, people began to take more serious steps to protect the condor. The government set aside national forest land as a condor *sanctuary*.

And in 1939, the National Audubon Society paid a scientist to study condors. Carl Koford from the University of California watched the birds for years. He recorded their activities and took 3,500 pages of notes.

Koford wrote a book called *The California Condor.* He described the way condors blink, stretch, yawn, turn their heads, and walk. He also described their mating and nesting habitats. It was the most information ever collected about the California condor.

In the 1940s, more land was set aside for the condor. But in the 1960s, another study by the National Audubon

Society found that there were only 40 condors left in the wild. It also found that most people still knew very little about condors. And they still did not know of the laws protecting the birds.

Part of the problem was that people could not agree on how to save the condor. Some environmental groups, such as the Sierra Club, felt that the best way to save the bird was to keep its habitat safe.

A prominent California rancher, Eben McMillan, agreed. He said the condor's plight was a warning signal from the environment. The way to take care of wildlife was to take care of the environment, he argued.

Some experts wanted to capture some of the birds and try to boost their numbers by breeding them in captivity. Critics said the birds were too sensitive and wouldn't breed in zoos.

Finally, in 1975, the first plan to save the condor was published. It called for a combination of wild birds and captive birds. It also recommended that the birds be sent back to their natural habitats once their numbers were higher.

The plan was the first rescue program for an endangered species since Congress passed the Endangered Species Act in 1973.

It wasn't going to be easy. Condors had not been hatched or *conceived* in captivity. No one knew whether the program would work.

People argued about the plan for years. They wondered whether a bird raised in a cage could survive in the wild.

Condor scientists added to the controversy when they entered a condor nest to weigh and measure a chick. It was one of only two chicks known to exist at that time. The chick grew alarmed when it was handled by a scientist. Its head sagged, and it collapsed. An *autopsy* showed that the bird had died from shock. The captive breeding plan came to a sudden halt.

In 1982, scientists started fitting condors in the wild with solar-powered radio transmitters. They hoped to learn more about the bird this way.

But in 1985, several of the remaining condors in the wild disappeared. Only a few were left. The government ordered the rest captured.

On Easter Sunday in 1987, the last wild condor, an adult male, was captured and brought to San Diego, California. Scientists caught him with a net while he fed on the carcass of a goat.

At that time, only 27 California condors existed in the world.

CHAPTER FOUR:

April 29, 1988, was a big day at the San Diego Wild Animal Park.

"Named Molloko, the Maidu Indian word for condor, an ungainly chick, 6.75 ounces, pecked its way out of its

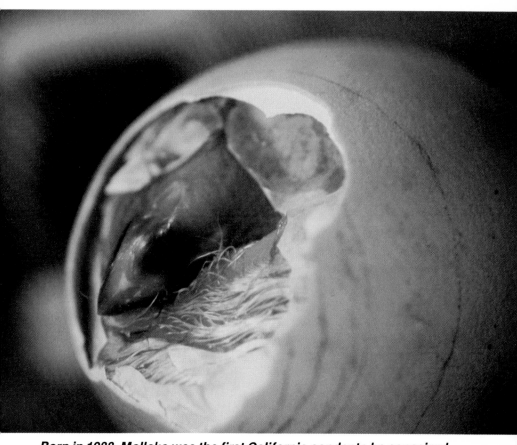

Born in 1988, Molloko was the first California condor to be conceived successfully in captivity.

shell to become the newest member of the embattled clan —and the first California condor ever conceived in captivity."

That was how *Time* magazine announced the condor chick's birth.

A special chick

Molloko's birth came about a year after the last wild condor was captured. It was a milestone and the news ran in newspapers and magazines around the country.

The number of California condors rose to 28. The birds were divided between the San Diego Wild Animal Park and the Los Angeles Zoo.

Molloko hatched to the sound of tape-recorded hissing and grunting noises. While her vision was still blurry, keepers fed her by hand. They held up her head and fed her with their fingers. After a few days, Molloko ate from the mouth of a condor puppet. Keepers used the puppet to keep the chick from thinking that a human was its parent.

Molloko ate 70 minced mice a day for her first meals. Later, keepers added turkey vulture vomit to her diet. It does not sound appetizing. But keepers wanted to try to copy the kind of food chicks get from their parents in the wild. The food from a vulture's gut contains important digestive bacteria as well as nourishment.

In the spring of 1989, four more condor chicks hatched. The births were a hopeful sign for the species and the captive breeding program.

This is how California condor chicks spend their childhood now. For the first two months, the chicks live in an *incubator*. They see humans for about five minutes a week. The chicks are weighed at that time.

34 *Keepers at the San Diego Wild Animal Park use puppets that look like condors to feed the chicks.*

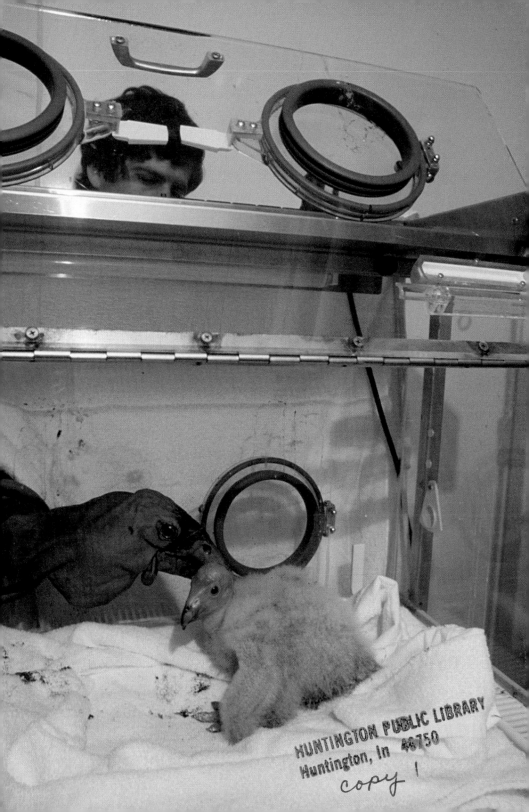

At two months, they are hooded and moved to a larger enclosure with a dirt floor. It is about eight feet by ten feet, the size of a small room. The chicks can see other condors from the enclosure. They are still fed with the puppet.

The next time they see people is at four to six months, when each bird gets a blood test. The test tells scientists whether the bird is male or female.

When the bird learns to fly, keepers move it to a *flight* with about five other juveniles. The flight is an enclosure that measures 40 feet by 80 feet by 28 feet, the size of a very large house.

The flight sits on a hilltop covered with rocks and natural chaparral. It is made of tall wooden poles with metal mesh draped over them.

At the San Diego Wild Animal Park, there are eight flights, four on each side of a long building. Keepers watch the birds from the building through one-way glass.

The park limits how often the condors see humans. The public cannot come within 300 yards of the condors' flights. The park won't even allow photographers to get near.

So far, the park hasn't let condor parents raise their own young. When a newly laid egg is taken from a female condor, she will often lay another to replace it. This is called *double-clutching*. California condors in the wild sometimes laid a second egg if the first was destroyed. Chicks will be born at a faster rate if the condors are encouraged to double-clutch.

After a young condor learns to fly, it is moved to a large open space called a flight. Keepers observe the bird through one-way glass.

Another reason the park separates parents from eggs is to keep the eggs safe. Condor parents at the Los Angeles Zoo laid an egg, were allowed to stay with it, and broke it.

At San Diego, a male condor leaped at a newly laid egg and struck it. It looked as if he were trying to break it. The park removed the egg.

The same pair laid another egg. This time the park re-

After a female has laid an egg, a keeper takes the egg to prompt the female to lay another one.

placed it with a dummy egg. Later, the park replaced the dummy egg with an Andean condor egg. The South American bird is more common. There are still a few thousand in the world, so the park's staff was more willing to risk the Andean condor egg.

The birds hatched the egg and the park's staff watched the birds raise the chick. It was a valuable experience because scientists had seen little of that when the birds were in the wild.

When the birds are released, scientists will compare chicks raised by puppets with chicks raised by condor parents. If the parent-raised birds do better in the wild than the puppet-raised birds, the park will change its program.

The 1989 births brought the total number of California condors to 32. Fourteen of them were at the Los Angeles Zoo. Eighteen were at the San Diego Wild Animal Park.

Thirty-two members of a species is not very many, but it is a reversal of a long, downhill slide.

A day in the life

Once a condor at the San Diego Wild Animal Park reaches breeding age, keepers pair it up with an unrelated member of the opposite sex.

Except at breeding time, the birds tend to keep to themselves. What they do during the day depends a little on the weather. If it is cool, they come out of their roost boxes when the sun comes out. If it is too hot, the birds will stay in the shade.

Keepers feed the birds through a trapdoor. The birds eat horsemeat, beef, or fish. The meat is left out long enough to spoil, just the way condors like it.

Once in a while, keepers will not feed the birds for a day. In the wild, condors sometimes go several days without food. The "fast days" keep the birds familiar with that habit.

Once in a while, the birds fly down from their roosts to drink from a pool or bathe. They tug at carcasses or branches during the day.

All day and every day, someone keeps track of what the birds do. Observers record up to 150 different types of condor behavior. This detailed record will help scientists understand the birds better.

The birds' life now is not the same as it was in the wild. But it is keeping the species alive. For example, in 1983, two condor eggs were taken from the wild. They hatched in captivity at the San Diego Wild Animal Park. One was a male, one was a female. Six years later, the two birds began courting, and keepers hope that someday they will produce an egg.

The two birds are a sign that life goes on for the California condor.

CHAPTER FIVE:

Scientists worry that not enough California condors survived to produce a healthy population. In 1987, the California condor population reached its lowest point at 27 birds. Was it enough to keep the species alive? So far, no one knows.

Too few to make it?

Condors, like all living things, carry the blueprint for their characteristics in the *genes*. The larger the pool of genes, the better the chances for success.

The biggest concern scientists have is that the *gene pool* for the California condor is too small. Many of the condors in San Diego and Los Angeles are brothers and sisters. They cannot be paired for breeding.

If scientists pair up related birds for breeding, defects may result. Some signs of *inbreeding* in a bird are infertility (inability to bear young), mouth breathing, stooping, and a loose tuck of its wings.

To add to the suspense, signs of inbreeding may not show up for a few generations. For now, scientists encourage the birds to lay eggs as fast as possible. If scientists are lucky, a larger flock of healthy condors will emerge.

Test fliers

In August 1988, the U.S. Fish and Wildlife Service released several Andean condor chicks into the California wilderness. All were females and all were bred in captivity.

The purpose was to test places to release the California

condor someday. If the Andean condors succeed in those areas, it means the California condor might also succeed later on.

The Andean condors were three months old and still covered with fuzzy down when they were brought to the release site. They were kept in large cages. The Fish and Wildlife Service felt it was important to place the birds in the wild at a very young age. Birds will *imprint* on an area, or fix it in their minds and memories, when they are young.

Scientists tagged the birds with tiny radio transmitters and someone watched them day and night. Observers tried to stay hidden from the birds to keep them from growing tame. They left food out at night for the birds to eat during the day.

The young birds started flying and were released when they were seven months old.

Already, a few of the birds have died. One chick died from stress. Later, a bird died after flying into a power line.

After two years of watching the birds, scientists will take the surviving Andean condors to Colombia, South America. The Colombian government wants to help increase the bird's range in its native continent.

Two California condors begin their courtship at the San Diego Wild Animal Park.

Free in the future?

In 1989, three more pairs of adult California condors began courting each other at the San Diego Wild Animal Park. Six pairs of condors were now breeding partners.

Condor keepers hope for eight to ten more fertile eggs in 1990.

Scientists hope to have enough birds by 1992 to release them into their former habitats. Perhaps they will go to nesting sites proven to be good by their cousins, the Andean condors.

Protected condor country in California today covers about 70,000 acres. The largest areas are in the Los Padres National Forest. The protected country also includes several wildlife refuges.

The state of California and private owners also have bought or set aside smaller pieces of land for the condor. Compared to the bird's former range, 70,000 acres is not much.

Some government experts think the nesting and roosting habitat on public land in the mountains will be safe for the birds when they return. The feeding areas on private grasslands may not be as safe.

The hazards that killed the condor in the wild remain. Power lines, land developers and industry, lead bullets, and pesticides still exist.

Many questions also remain. For example, the government is providing carcasses for the experimental Andean condors to eat. Should they provide safe food for the California condor, too? If they do, the birds may not need to cross as much dangerous ground to search for food. They may learn to feed in a much smaller, safer area.

Will the California condor be tame when it is released? Will inbreeding cripple the species?

Efforts to save the California and the Andean condors (above) will continue until the birds are no longer in danger of extinction.

The effort to save the condor was controversial. And the program today is expensive. It costs up to $1 million a year. Most people agree that the bird's survival is important. The condor is a living link to the past. We can learn much about survival and conditions of ancient times from the condor.

Dick Smith, author of *California Condor, Vanishing American,* wrote, "The condor had become a symbol in the critical relationship between man and nature. The bird is like the canary in the coal mine. If he [the bird] languishes, can the environment be healthy for other living creatures, including man?"

When there are 200 California condors back in the wild, and when births equal or exceed deaths, the captive breeding program is scheduled to shut down.

Until then, no one will know whether this gamble to save a bird succeeded.

INDEX/GLOSSARY: